small stations fiction

Xabier P. DoCampo

When There's a Knock
on the Door at Night

Published in 2018 by
SMALL STATIONS PRESS
20 Dimitar Manov Street, 1408 Sofia, Bulgaria
You can order books and contact the publisher at
www.smallstations.com

This book was first published in the Galician language as *Cando petan na porta pola noite* by Edicións Xerais de Galicia (Vigo, 1994). A list of our fiction titles can be found at www.smallstations.com/fiction

This work received a grant from the General Secretariat of Culture of the Ministry of Culture, Education and University Planning of the Xunta de Galicia in the call for translation grants of the year 2017

Esta obra recibiu unha axuda da Secretaría Xeral de Cultura da Consellería de Cultura, Educación e Ordenación Universitaria da Xunta de Galicia na convocatoria de axudas para a tradución do ano 2017

ISBN 978-954-384-087-8

Xabier P.
DoCampo

When There's a Knock on the Door at Night

WINNER
OF THE
SPANISH NATIONAL
BOOK AWARD FOR
YOUNG PEOPLE'S
LITERATURE

Translated from Galician by **Jonathan Dunne**

Small Stations Press

for Raimundo and Teresa,
my parents, in memoriam

Contents

Author's Note

The stories I like best are those that came into being in order to be told orally; those whose essence it is to turn into air and the sound that comes out of the mouth of a woman or a man telling a story. That is why, in these stories, there is a lot of memory and tribute to my father, who was a great storyteller.

I received so many stories by word of mouth that my soul is full of them. Stories that were told to me and that settled down to rest there. Stories like the ones I include here, which made me go to bed on many nights with fear; I would struggle to keep my eyes open and watch how the moonlight eased the darkness of the room; that slender light drove away my fear, and this enabled me to become master of the territory I was in. The secret was not to let myself be carried away to that other territory inhabited by monsters.

But I had a trick for this. The fear only lasted the time it took for me to take possession of the story, to make it mine and to add it to my collection of stories, that nest in my soul where they would cease to be foreign stories, because I made them mine, and would no longer scare me. How could I possibly be afraid of something that was now mine?

That is how the stories I include here came about. They are stories that were born and raised in that nest of the soul, but they are made from materials that came in through my ears, entered into contact with one another and permitted me to bear this fruit I now present to you, the reader.

Enjoy them without fear, even if they seem a little frightening. I hope some of them may nest in your own soul and turn into your own stories. Tell them, then, taking possession of the greatest good you will ever inherit: the word. This is what a human has that is most human, together with the capacity to tell stories that intermesh until they generate this enormous network of stories that are all similar and all completely different, depending on the person who tells them, because anyone who tells a story has of necessity first passed it through his soul and made it his own.

Xabier P. DoCampo
March 1994

The Traveller's Mirror

It had been

a day of constant rain. A cold, thin rain that only ever stopped to give way to hail or snow. A better night could hardly be expected after such a day, rather quite the opposite, and that is how it was. But now there was a blustery wind as well that made walking a laborious and unpleasant task. I had to get off the horse and lead it by the reins because the animal, disoriented by the air and water, wouldn't let itself be guided through the blackness of that night without the slightest hint of moon. Whereas before it was the horse that kept stumbling, threatening to throw me off, now I was the one that kept staggering this way and that, so that only the horse's strength and my hands clinging to the reins prevented me from doing worse than falling on my knees in the mud from time to time.

In the morning, when I had set out, I had reckoned it would take me only two days to reach my destination, and not even the absence of seven years traversing those roads had managed to divert me one foot from the correct path. But that was during the daytime, which, though dark and unpleasant, had allowed me to progress with a certain sense of security. Now I was absolutely certain that I was lost and all I wanted was to find some shelter for the night before I strayed a long way from the path.

I attempted to walk with my head next to the horse's in order to protect myself from the air and water. I wandered like this for a long time, until in the distance it seemed to me I could make out a light. Whether or not it was a light, I headed in that direction. As time went by, I became more and more certain that it wasn't a product of my imagination because it kept on reappearing whenever the detours I was obliged to take on account of the rough terrain made me lose sight of it. It certainly wasn't a ghost because it remained motionless all the while.

It wasn't long before I was sufficiently close to the light to realize it came from inside a house. Once I descended the hill I was on, only a smallish chestnut grove would stand between me and its front door.

Having left behind the last of the chestnut trees, barely twenty feet from the house, I moved towards the enormous front door, the top half of which was open and filled with a blinding light that seemed to me to be emanating from the gates of paradise, however much, as I had been approaching, I had been convinced the glare proceeded from the flames of hell itself.

I peered through the opening and finally discovered what fire it was causing so much light: a blacksmith's forge.

I tied my beast to a hitching ring and knocked hard on the door with the stick I was carrying, while at the same time shouting out, '*Laus Deo!*'

The occupant of the house must have been standing right by the door because in a flash a face appeared that came close to mine and which I couldn't make out in the darkness of the night.

'May he always be praised! Come in, draw near to the fire, it's not a night for wandering outside,' he said while opening the door.

I entered the room, which was open plan and where, apart from the forge, there was a fireplace with a blackened bench, a good-sized trough surrounded by three or four chairs and a large pantry. On the other side of the forge, behind the bellows, an arched doorway revealed the smithy, which was piled high with single- and double-headed anvils, tongs, pokers and all the paraphernalia you would expect to find in a blacksmith's house. An open door revealed a staircase that hugged the left wall and led to the upper floor.

Walking in front of the owner of the house, I approached the fireplace, hearing his voice all the while, which encouraged me to sit close to the fire so I could get dry while he himself offered to shelter and unharness my horse. I sat down on the bench in front of the fire and watched as my host left the house.

It didn't take him long to reappear with an armful of wood, which he tossed on the fire. He grabbed a stool and sat down opposite me. It was then I could properly examine his features for the first time, and I almost fell backwards in surprise: his face was in all respects almost identical to mine. The only difference was in his left eye. To start with, it seemed much bigger than the other. It then occurred to me this was because he had opened it more than the right one. After a while, I saw it never blinked. And finally I realized it was because his left eye had no eyelid. I gazed in amazement at this face, as if looking at myself in the mirror while making unpleasant gestures with my right eye, it was so similar in all respects to mine: the same pale, sparse hair on the crown, the same pointy, somewhat aquiline nose, the same thin-lipped mouth, the same broad chin… It felt like a nightmare and I did nothing to disguise my amazement as he carried on watching me, apparently unaware of the likeness in our appearance, in our very own identity. He seemed to ignore this fact to such an extent that, when he started talking, I didn't dare remark on it.

He told me he was a blacksmith and on nights like this he lit a huge fire in the forge so lost travellers like me would have a light to guide them. I told him I was on my way back to my house, which I had left seven years before, and was coming back to take over the small inheritance my parents, now deceased, had left me.

When I was dry, the man produced some food from the pantry, which he placed on the table so I could have supper. He didn't accompany me, except for the wine, which we drank in such large quantities that the man with the lidless eye often had to leave the house with an empty jug in order to return with a full one.

I gradually lost the awkwardness I had initially felt on noting the remarkable similarity between the two of us.

We talked of all those things one talks about on nights of wine. We repeatedly fell into heated arguments and more than once dealt each other blows and shoves. On one occasion I grabbed my knife and held it towards him. He leaped around and grabbed a poker sticking out of the forge. We both found it tremendously difficult to stand on our own two feet and let out enormous guffaws, facing off, me with the knife and him parading the poker in front of my eyes. I made a lunge with the knife as if to frighten him, but just as I was expecting him to take a step backwards in order to avoid the thrust, he leaped towards me and aimed the red-hot poker at my left eye. I let out the largest, ugliest shout my throat was capable of producing…

I don't know how long it was before I woke up. I was in bed and could feel no pain. I passed my hand over my face and realized it was bandaged. A cloth went under my left ear all the way around my head, covering the eye on that side. Over the eye, I could feel the bandage was thicker. The bed was obviously upstairs, in one of the corners, the one on the left-hand side as you came up the stairs. In the middle of the room was a large table and, behind it, a sideboard. In the wall opposite the bed was a window with open shutters. Beneath the window, a washbasin on an iron stand. Opposite the sideboard and table, a wooden partition with a closed door in it.

It wasn't long before the blacksmith arrived. He was carrying a bowl of light broth, which he placed on a stool next to my bed. He started giving me an explanation before I had a chance to ask him for one. He said it had all been an unfortunate consequence of the wine. It seemed he also had been wounded; he showed me a stab wound in his stomach, which had already started to heal. He revealed he himself had treated my eye, although, however much I asked him, he wouldn't go into details as to the likely consequences for my eye. All he said was that he was particularly skilled at such labours and many neighbours from far and wide sought him out to cure their wounds.

He wouldn't let me out of bed all that day or the three that followed. He lavished me with attention and hardly left me alone. He stayed at my side, telling me all sorts of things about his life. Whenever I insisted on getting up and continuing my journey, he would say there was no hurry, it was he who had wounded me and he couldn't let me leave his house until I was completely recovered. So it was I found out he had a wife, who was away at the moment and wouldn't be back any time soon because she had gone to look after her old, sick father.

I started to feel like a prisoner who is not allowed to move without permission. Whenever I tried to get out of bed, he would appear out of nowhere and stop me. He seemed to have some kind of warning system that enabled him to distinguish the sounds of the mattress when I turned over in bed from those that showed I was trying to get up. I reached the conclusion he could discern my intentions because, whenever I made another attempt to get to my feet, the blacksmith would turn up and convince me to go back to lying down.

Finally, one night, he announced I could get up the very next day.

When I saw the daylight filtering through the cracks in the shutters, I leaped out of bed. I ran towards the window, tearing off the bandages as I went. Behind the shutter, just above the washbasin, I had seen a little mirror, but when I looked for it, it wasn't there. I went to open the window so I could see myself in the panes of glass against the shutter. I don't know how or why, but the window no longer had any panes in it.

At that precise moment, the blacksmith came upstairs and, before saying anything, I asked him for a mirror. He replied the devil take him, but there wasn't one in the whole house. However much I told him I wanted to see what my face looked like and, even if it was bad, I wouldn't hold it against him, it had obviously been a wine-induced accident, I couldn't get him to stop coming out with the excuse that it so happened there wasn't a mirror in the house.

I cupped some water from the basin and searched in its depths, hoping to see my face. All I could make out was the dark silhouette of my head, without being able to see enough to work out what my appearance was like after the accident.

All day, I went about, searching for something that would reflect my face with sufficient clarity to reveal my appearance. The blacksmith and I hardly said a word to each other the whole time. He was almost always busy in the smithy, while I was searching for my image.

The next day, when I got up, I remembered my horse had been in the stables for a long time and I still hadn't been to see him, this animal I loved so much, who was such a loyal friend to me. I headed towards the stables and found him clean and well nourished. It was clear the blacksmith had looked after him well all the days I had spent in bed. Over an empty manger was my saddle and the horse's tackle. A noticeable gleam emanated from the bridle bit. I grabbed it and wiped it on the sleeve of my shirt. Little daylight penetrated the stables, so I went outside. I rubbed the bit vigorously on my shirt and held it in front of my face. The first thing I saw was my mouth. I moved it and succeeded in contemplating my nose. My anxiety made me handle the shining piece of metal a little carelessly, and the next thing I saw were the roots of my hair. A slight movement, and now I could see my eyes, deformed by the curvature of the mouthpiece. Here I could finally discern the results of our struggle and the blacksmith's surgery: my left eye was lacking an eyelid. Dear God! Now I really was identical in every way to that accursed blacksmith.

I spent a long while sitting on a stone, gazing from time to time at my face on the bit. I kept seeing the blacksmith's face. My heart slowly filled with rage. This hadn't been an accident! It had all been prepared beforehand! The wine, the fight, he'd thought it all out so I would be like him. He'd probably wounded himself in the stomach to make that nonsense about an accident sound more plausible. My blood was thumping in my temples, while hate surged forcibly through me.

I went back inside the house and didn't say a word. In the days that followed, I continued accepting his attention as if nothing was wrong. Meanwhile, I kept an eye on all his movements so I could work out the best time to carry out my revenge. On the few occasions we were face to face, I stared at his eye shamelessly. I had lost the sense of insecurity one has in front of a cripple, when it seems one's sight is constantly being drawn to the injury and one tries to look the other way. No, now I fixed my gaze on his lidless eye insolently and didn't take it away until he had turned around.

The blacksmith slept on a bed of straw next to the hearth and continued giving me the bed upstairs. One night, I confirmed how trusting he had become because, even though I got out of bed four times, he never made a sound downstairs to make me think he'd woken up. The following night, I had a go at climbing up and down the stairs without him waking up; I even stood less than a foot away from where he was sleeping, and he didn't flinch! The rage in my chest advanced at the same rate as my plans for killing him.

That day, I selected a weapon from the smithy that struck me as most appropriate: a heavy, sharp chopping knife. I hid it under my clothes and managed to steal it upstairs. I then placed it under the mattress.

I waited impatiently for night to come. I felt no fear at the idea of committing a crime; actually, I could hardly wait for the moment to arrive. There was no trace of doubt or mercy inside my heart, just an overriding desire to deprive that demoniacal being of life. I was sure that, having done so, I would feel perfectly well, without the slightest hint of remorse.

At nightfall, my idea was to wait for him to lie down next to the hearth so I could go up to bed, but he didn't stop wandering about. He went in and out of the smithy for no apparent reason. As usual, we barely said a word to each other. So I headed for the stairs and tucked myself into bed. From there, I could hear how he spread some straw on the floor in order to lie down. I waited long enough for the blacksmith to have fallen asleep and then got up. The memory of his light sleep that had made him turn up beside my bed every time I moved encouraged me to stay still for a while, having got out of bed. Nothing. He didn't budge. I went downstairs, making as little noise as if I was walking on air. The door between the stairs and the kitchen was half closed. I pushed it gently, and it opened without making a sound. I was expecting this since during the day, taking advantage of the blacksmith's absence, I had been careful to lubricate its hinges.

There he was, lying in front of the hearth. The bulk of his body was illuminated by the embers of the forge. He was facing the hearthstone, with his back to the room. I crept up cautiously. Every step, I paused to see if my breathing was enough to wake him.

After that, I was next to him. He was completely covered by a blanket. All you could see was the form of a man lying down. It was then that my brain was assailed by doubt. What if he suspected my intentions, and this lump was nothing but a handful of straw covered in a blanket? What if he was right behind me at this very moment, watching me approach with a chopper in my hand? Should I look around in case he jumped on me with a sledgehammer and dealt me a death blow instead? Or perhaps I should retreat, put my plans off until the following night? I couldn't even make out the rise and fall of his breathing! The blood pounded in my temples so much I thought they would burst.

But another idea came into my mind: there was no going back. I couldn't change my mind, having got this far. If this shape was not the blacksmith's body, then he could see that I was next to him, holding a weapon with which to do him in. I raised the chopper and dealt the first blow where I thought his head should be. A sound like that of treading on dry leaves. I raised my arm again while pulling back the blanket with my left hand. There was the blacksmith's dented head. I turned his body over so that it was facing upwards. His lidless eye fixed its rotten gaze on my own lidless organ. I dealt a second blow with the chopper, and his eye burst before the weapon could sink in as far as the handle.

I peppered that head with many more blows. By the time I had finished, there was no face left. It wasn't like looking at myself in the mirror anymore. I sat down on the hearthstone, panting from the effort.

Having got my breath back, I grabbed a hoe and a shovel and dug a deep, well-formed hole in the back garden, where I buried the blacksmith's body. I then chucked the bloodstained straw into the fire of the forge and cleaned the kitchen carefully.

Dawn found me still at my labours. All I had to do was harness my horse and get the hell out of there. I was just about to do this when I heard the sound of people outside. I peeped through the top half of the door and saw two people heading towards the house. One was on horseback, the other was walking alongside. They had left the chestnut grove behind them and would soon be at the front door. I realized I was still in my nightshirt. I grabbed the blacksmith's clothes and put them on. I went over to the forge and started working the bellows.

It didn't take them long to come in through the door. One was a woman of more or less my own age; the other was a boy of about twenty. They started talking to me, as if unfazed by my presence. I don't know what they were saying. My head was spinning! I only paid attention to them from time to time. It turned out the woman's father had died. This woman was the blacksmith's wife and seemed to think I was her husband! It wasn't long before another man turned up, wanting to shoe his horse, and he also took me for the blacksmith.

They were all talking to me as if I was the blacksmith I had just killed. That was enough to drive anybody crazy! I was about to shout at them that I'd just killed the blacksmith and was a traveller on his way home. They carried on talking to me as if I was the blacksmith. I started saying yes, no, we'll see... I also was beginning to fill the space left by the dead blacksmith. I had committed a crime, and this was my sentence: to live out the life I had taken from the blacksmith!

The Oven Man

'Are you going to tell me what happened to the Oven Man?'

This is what I asked my father one day when we were heading from Castro to Roás. He looked at me and laughed, possibly because he hadn't been expecting the question, he had no idea I would be so interested in something that had happened so many aeons before, but I rather think his laughter was caused by his belief that I was planning to write something about this famous episode.

I was right, his reply confirmed it to me:

'I'll tell you everything I know about this story if you like, but you'd better not write it down. You know we're almost related to his family, and I don't think they'd like seeing it in the papers, especially if it's written by you!'

I confess I didn't promise not to do this. Rather I would say I gave him to understand the exact opposite. I must have said something like, 'While you're alive, I won't do it,' something like that, because he seemed to agree and I felt I was in a position to hear a story I could then write down. I don't have the feeling I'm breaking any sort of promise.

The old man settled into his car seat, stopped looking at me and fixed his eyes on the road, the infinite or not outside, but on his memory, as he liked to do. He then started talking as was his wont: relishing the narrative, he liked nothing better than to tell stories.

'The story's an old one, but there are still plenty of people living now who remember it perfectly well. Those who were somehow involved deny it; others claim it happened in exactly the way it has been told. I can only say that a story for which somebody paid a year or two in prison must have happened one way or the other, the guilty party may have gone to prison or somebody else may have paid the price, but if there are dead people in the middle and they didn't die of natural causes, then the fact is somebody must have killed them.

'It all happened right about here,' we were just coming into Xermar, 'and it was all on account of this old woman. A damnable old woman, I can tell you now she was one of the worst people that ever walked this planet, barring those who were responsible for the death of Our Lord. Her tongue was as sharp as a cobra's. There was no house, no reputation, she set her lips or eyes on that wasn't poisoned forever thereafter. Don't think I'm claiming she was a witch and inflicted evil by practising arts not all of us possess. No, hers was a common sort of evil. She used no other weapon than that you or I might wield: the word. But she lacked the slightest hint of charity, morals, respect for the reputations of others, all those things that make the rest of us curtail our speech, not share every thought that comes into our minds and certainly not dare to relate things we know nothing about or, even worse, heap malicious rumours on other people's lives.

'But the wretchedness of this old woman didn't stop there because, while she was putting her tongue out to graze, she would also go about shifting boundaries, pulling down walls, diverting streams, all the kinds of tricks someone could play in a country like ours, only she would do and undo them a hundredfold.

'She didn't seem to care that nobody in the parish loved her, that concerned her just about as much as what was going on in Cuba. So one day three full-grown men, all victims of the woman's actions, themselves or their families, decided the time had come to teach this old woman a lesson, given there was no justice, human or divine, that would make her modify her behaviour the tiniest bit.

'Having made up their minds, they decided the best way to put the old woman in her place was to give her a good hiding without offering any further explanation than the whipping itself. They were convinced both she and they would be perfectly aware of the causes and reasons behind the beating they proposed to inflict on her, but they were far less sure said beating would do anything to change the woman's concept of cohabitation with her neighbours, the first time would be a test run, it might have to be repeated, they would have to see...

'They waited until night had put everybody in their houses and then set off for the old woman's dwelling. I don't need to tell you they weren't carrying weapons of any kind, each of them laid hold of something with which to carry out the job in the old woman's yard: one grabbed an upright from the cart, another took a goad made of hazel, while the third dismantled an axe and made for the house with the handle in his hand. They reached the door, had a go at the upper half and found it was bolted from inside. The one with the upright put a hand inside the frame of the window above the drain and broke the lock at the second attempt, a third push, and the handle snapped, releasing the window. They swept into the kitchen and ran towards the staircase. The first was just about to set foot on the bottom step when the old woman came shouting down the stairs, dressed in an old and stained burlap nightshirt. The one with the hazel goad advanced towards her, so she turned around and dashed back upstairs. At that precise moment, a blow landed on her back, running down the length of her spine. She let out a shout that didn't seem to come from this world and carried on running. The old woman was just setting foot on the upper floor when the three men leaped up the stairs, two at a time. They all arrived together, and the old woman jumped on top of her bed. The light of the moon let it be known to them that she was planning to seek refuge between the bed and the wall, so one of the men took hold of her calf and pulled. The woman was sprawled on top of the bed, her crumpled nightshirt up around her waist. That was when they started beating the old woman. The upright and the axe handle rained down on the old woman's body, which let out sounds as if bones were breaking. The hazel goad whistled through the air before making contact with the old woman's soft buttocks and eliciting the most petrifying screams.

'They beat the old woman until they could do no more. Without a word, the one with the goad let go of her calf and the one with the upright stopped flogging that body that had ceased to have feelings some time before. The axe handle was still raised when the old woman, on being released, turned face upwards. At that precise moment, the handle came down and landed smack in the middle of the woman's forehead. They heard her skull break, out came a trickle of blood, and the old woman opened wide her eyes. She fixed them on the eyes of the man holding the handle as if they were two red-hot irons and said, "I'll make you sorry for this, Teixo, even if I die." The three of them legged it downstairs. They dropped their implements in the yard outside and ran away.

'Not long afterwards, the three of them were in the kitchen of Teixo's house. They were panting like dogs that have just been involved in the race of their lives. I didn't see them, but I can imagine they were staring at the floor between their feet without daring to look at one another. The fact is they must have discussed the question of whether the old woman was dead or not and, in order to find this out, the only option was to head back the way they had come. "I'm not going," "You can go," "Forget about it," the fact is somebody had to do it, and that person was Teixo. It didn't take him long to retrace his steps: the old woman was dead, well dead and growing cold.

'There was no way they planned to come clean about the murder, so what they did was hitch the oxen to the cart, wrap the old woman in her bedspread and lay her in the back. There was still plenty of night left, and it can't have been more than half a league to Escanavada. There was a communal oven there that was far away from the houses and hadn't been used in years.

'I've heard it said the only sound along the way was that of the oxen's hooves and the wooden wheels on the pebbles. They reached the oven in just over an hour. They threw in some dry gorse and the old woman's stiff body. Then they lit the oven. The gorse caught fire, the flames clambered all over the bedspread. At the foot of the oven door, they watched as the old woman became naked and the noxious smell of burnt hair infiltrated their nostrils. Now that the fire had conquered the old woman's body, it wouldn't be long before it burned, although I read not long ago that bodies burn badly, especially bones; that said, I tend to agree with what the three of them must have been thinking: if there's fire enough, excepting stones, there are few things that won't burn.

'In effect, the fire took hold of the old woman, the flames started emitting blue and green hues. The smell of scorched flesh isn't exactly what we would call a perfume, but they stayed where they were, in front of the oven door, watching the spectacle. They felt a bit calmer now that the body had disappeared and, seeing nobody would hear from the old woman, it wouldn't take the story long to die down.

'What the three of them couldn't do was take their eyes off the fire that enveloped her body. One of them, I don't know who, declared, "Let her burn and the devil

take her, that'll give him one hell here and another there."
No sooner had he said this than the old woman sat bolt
upright inside the oven. She folded down the middle and
sat there, her eyes wide open, fixed on Teixo's. The three
of them went stiff as spindles. But in less time than it
takes to tell you, they turned and legged it through the
front door. One of them shouted, "Damn that woman and
the one that brought her into existence!" Teixo looked
back just as the old woman slowly raised her arm and
pointed at him while baring her teeth. The poor old oxen
endured blows to make them quicken their pace more
than an ox is supposed to.

'A little further on, they stopped and started saying they
couldn't just leave the old woman in the oven, but they
weren't prepared to go back and so, convinced the flames
would finally consume the old woman's body, they each
headed home.

'For two or three days, nobody missed the old woman,
and nothing was said. But on the fourth day the civil
guards turned up and started asking questions. It was
no secret that the three men had resolved to give the old
woman a beating, so they took them to Lugo and put them
in prison. When the case came before the court, it was
Teixo who took the fall. I can't remember now whether
he spent one year, or two, in prison, but it wasn't such a
long period of time. Having completed his sentence, he
returned to his house, and the story would have ended
there, had it not been for the rest of it.

'After that, people no longer referred to "Teixo" when
talking about him, from that moment onwards he was

known as the "Oven Man", they even came up with a song for him:

With another two, Oven Man
went to cook an old woman in an oven
there is over in Escanavada.
The oven was still warm,
the woman half baked,
when she turned her attention towards them.
They legged it through the air,
got the hell out of there,
the baking unfinished.
What a funny thing
for someone who doesn't even know how to cook
to be called the Oven Man.

'That said, I don't know of anyone who would have sung this ditty to his face. When he came back, he was smug, even proud of what he'd done, but it didn't take him long to become more withdrawn, and his family and neighbours found it increasingly difficult to communicate with him. He would spend days shut up at home, and then he suddenly took to wandering from place to place and sleeping out in the lee of walls.

'Many years later, I was on my way from Arcilla to Xermar, it was getting dark and, as I passed through Lamas, I saw him huddled up against a stone. I went up to him and greeted him. He was thin and pockmarked, but he must have felt like talking to somebody because he slid down the stone until he was sitting on the ground and invited me to do the same. I don't recall what we talked about before he started telling me his story. From that point on, it was he who did the talking, I was too amazed to interrupt him. This is what he told me.

"'More than anything,' said the Oven Man, 'I'd be grateful if you'd put your hands around my neck and strangle me here and now, I know it doesn't sound like a good death, but the way things are I'd prefer that to what is happening. I know you'll say all I have to do is kill myself, and that'll be the end of it, but it's not so easy, as you'll find out. You realize, like everybody else, that I killed the old woman and we went to burn her in the oven at Escanavada. I know it was me who killed her because, although we all beat her black and blue, she is convinced it was me and won't stop making me pay for it. Not a day goes by she doesn't come to exact some form of payment. She was a wretch in life, as few have been, but now she's dead, she's even more so. You may not believe me when I tell you this, but I see that old woman every day. To start with, it seemed it would be enough for me to pay my debt to justice, and I accepted this: I had committed a murder and would have to pay for it. But that accursed soul wasn't satisfied and, ever since I was released, she's been coming round to settle her own accounts.

"'The first time she did this was in the kitchen of my house. I was sitting by the fire and felt this heat rising up my back while at the same time I could hear panting behind me. I turned around, and there was the old woman immersed in flames, I don't know whether they were the flames of hell or those of the fire we lit, the fact is that devilish old woman was staring at me out of a fire-scorched face and baring her teeth. I was afraid, but then I thought this was just a vision, and visions and horror stories had never frightened me all that much, so I endeavoured to regain control of myself and wait to see what would happen. We looked at each other for a while until she spoke and said she would take me to hell with her, but she wanted us to be a single entity in that other place and so I would have to become an indivisible part of her. Of all she said, I didn't understand much at the time, but it didn't take me long to comprehend. At the time, I didn't stop to think about it, I looked around, grabbed a frying pan in both hands, walked over to the woman and whacked her over the head with all my might. She didn't even whimper. The same place she'd come in, letting off the heat of flames, there now entered the kitchen a blast of cold that surrounded my body and penetrated to my bones while at the same time the fire in the fireplace suddenly went out. I tried to light it again, but couldn't. I went off to bed, feeling frozen, and couldn't get to sleep. I kept on turning over, but time stayed still. I don't know what hour of the night it was, or how long I'd been in bed, when the room filled with this warm light. There was the old woman again. She walked towards me, saying, 'Today I'm going to eat one of your kidneys.' She carried on getting closer and, having reached the bed, stretched out an arm, placed her hand – bare bones with bits of smoking flesh hanging off the fingers – on my stomach and slipped inside me as a hot knife would slide through a slab of butter. I felt the most terrible pain

I have ever felt as the old woman's hand rummaged inside me. I closed my eyes and, when I opened them again, I saw that the woman's face was all bloody. Blood oozed from a piece of flesh she was eating and ran down her chin and onto her chest.

"'I spent the night with terrible pains as if a dozen crows were pecking at my flesh. At dawn, the pains subsided. I looked at my stomach and could see no sign of a wound. I still felt some discomfort, but it was no worse than what you get when you've eaten something bad, so I thought it must all have been a nightmare. It even occurred to me I may have felt some remorse for what we'd done to the old woman. I went down to the kitchen and there was the frying pan. I picked it up and was just about to put it back when I saw it had this dent in the bottom. That detail matched what had happened; I can assure you when I took it for the first time to defend myself against the woman, it had been as smooth as stone. There was another detail that seemed to fit: that day, I urinated blood.

"'I had been wondering whether it had all really happened or was just some kind of bad dream for a number of days when one night, on my way back from Mos, as I was crossing Ponte Vilar, I caught sight of the old woman again. To start with, all I saw was the light of the fire that goes with her because she jumped on top of me and pulled out my liver in less time than it takes to tell you. As I clutched my stomach in the midst of the worst pain a human being has ever had to suffer, she ate my organ as if it was some kind of delicacy. I shouted like crazy, out of pain and fear. I vomited and spat blood the whole night. As if it were a curse, nobody came to help me. I spent hours shouting and crying until dawn arrived to assuage my pain.

"'Another night, she visited the house and tore out my pancreas. The pain was getting more and more unbearable and, once I was finally able to get out of bed, I went to the shed and tried to hang myself with a rope, but the rope broke and the old woman came to tell me I wouldn't be able to take my own life, someone else would have to kill me, and then she would eat my heart.

"'I left the house and started wandering from place to place. I am living out the worst death a man could experience. I am almost empty on the inside, but she keeps on coming to rummage around in search of something else to tear out. Little by little, I am starting to form part of the old woman, and there's nowhere I can escape to. Two nights ago, I went and slept in the church in Ponte de Outeiro; I thought it being a sacred place, an infernal being wouldn't be able to enter there. She turned up in the middle of the night and stretched out her arm, I don't know what there was for her to take, there can't have been anything left, but still she stuck in her hand of bones and frazzled skin and fell to eating. She ate on top of the altar and from time to time spat in the direction of the sanctuary to demonstrate her contempt for all things holy, as if there was no place on earth where I could hide.

"'I don't know if I will find someone charitable enough to take my life and put an end to all this suffering. I don't even know if that's what I want because, if it's true what the old woman has told me, then I shall be joined to her forever in hell, suffering in my own flesh the punishment I am owed as well as that she has coming to her. I know you're not going to be able to help me, I don't even know why I've told you all this, I suppose it's so that people won't think I've gone crazy..."

'At this point, he got up from where we'd been half sitting, half squatting, and walked off, clinging to the stones. I sat there, watching him go, and saw how he leaped onto the path and headed towards the river. I soon had news of him. Four or five days later, he turned up dead in Triabá. Don Clemente came to remove the corpse and an autopsy was carried out in Castro de Rei cemetery. With the excuse that I was going to Santa Leocadia, I journeyed to Castro de Rei, went to see Don Clemente and asked him what the Oven Man had died of. Well, he'd died of a blow to the head, that was what it said in the coroner's report, but the doctor had told him he hadn't dared to write what he'd really found out during the autopsy in case he was considered incompetent or crazy: he had no other wound than that on his head, but inside he was completely empty. Hollowed out like a clog, like a pig, if you'll pardon the expression, that has had its guts and lungs removed!'

The She-Wolf

.

In my grandfather's house

in Granda de Xermar there was always a horse farm, and that is why, back in the 1930s, my father had to go several times to the horse farm there was in Reborica, which was the one that was closest and with which they had very good relations.

On one of those trips – I can't remember now whether the reason for it was the sale and delivery of a horse from the farm or the purchase of one of those Castilian donkeys that are as tall as horses and were so highly esteemed and expensive at that time when mare mules were worth a lot of money and were highly sought after, unlike their male counterparts, which weren't such active workers – he found out about a story he told me twenty-five or thirty years later, which I am now writing down.

My father used always to follow the same route, unless for some particular reason he had to take a diversion to Cambás, where we still have relatives, or to Xestoso, where my great-grandfather 'War' lived and was always being talked about, a man of immense strength that made him the leading character in tales and stories, some real, others invented. But this wasn't the case, so he crossed the Támoga and entered Pino. He skirted Mato, headed for Pígara and would soon have been in Santa Cruz de Parga, and from there in Trasparga, had it not begun to snow. It snowed heavily, and the snow began to settle in such a way there was a real threat of the paths disappearing from sight. He urged the horse on to see if he could get to Trasparga more quickly; from there Reborica was only a stone's throw away.

But things didn't turn out in quite the way my father had planned, the snowfall was one of those that linger in the memory. He crossed the river Requeixo over a rickety old bridge he could hardly make out in the midst of the snowstorm, and man and horse almost ended up in the water. Night fell suddenly, and there was no way of being sure which direction to go in. He dismounted and, taking the horse by the reins, stumbled about in search of tracks, hoping against hope that he would find a house where they could shelter for the night.

It wasn't easy, the disappearance of the paths meant man and horse wandered about in search of the most tenuous byways. When it snows at night, the flakes make you absolutely blind, and the most usual thing is to get lost if you don't come across shelter quickly; little by little, your chest fills with rage, which soon turns into unease, so that the difficulties inherent in the situation are made worse by your lack of a mental ability to resolve them. Something like this is what must have happened to my father that night. Having wandered this way and that, he glimpsed a little light that wasn't far away and headed towards it. He tried not to lose sight of it even when he had to turn around and go back the way he had come because he'd encountered an obstacle or a stream. He always searched for the light and directed his steps towards it. Shapes and forms all became round and looked alike as if there was the same thing inside them and the only difference was in the size.

With no little difficulty, he reached the edge of the threshing floor. He started to cross it, leading the horse by the reins. The dogs began to bark, and he had to calm the horse down, placing a hand on its lower lip and speaking softly to it, 'Easy now, easy now.' A figure appeared in the door of the house, and my father headed towards it.

'Good evening!' he said by way of greeting.

'Good evening to you, though I would hardly call it that! Tie your horse up and come in, it's not a night to be wandering about,' replied the silhouette, moving aside to leave the doorway clear.

My father secured the horse and went in, taking off the oilskin cape that had protected him from the elements. Without venturing much further than the threshold of the door, he explained his predicament and asked if he and the horse could be given shelter for the night. As expected, both requests were immediately granted, so he went back outside and shut the horse in a shed that was a little away from the house. He removed the saddle and dried the horse with the blanket before the man of the house arrived with an armful of barley, which he laid in front of the animal's muzzle.

Preceded by the man who had welcomed him and helped him to settle the horse, he entered the house. It was a farmhouse like any other, like the one he himself had come from. He entered the kitchen and said:

'Thank you kindly!'

'God be thanked,' replied a woman, stirring a pot with a handle that was hanging from a cross-beam. She must have been close to sixty, about the same age as the man who had shown him in. The greeting was then answered by the other inhabitants of the house, who were huddled around the fire. Sitting on stools, a girl of about eighteen or nineteen and a young boy of fourteen or something. On a blackened bench behind the fire, another, older woman who seemed to be fiddling about in the embers and ashes with a stick.

My father explained how he'd become lost on account of the snowstorm, where he was going and what for. So it was he found out he'd strayed a long way from the path and, instead of heading in the direction of the sunset, as he should have, at some point he'd veered north and was now in Vilargabín, a good distance from his road.

'Well, if you've come here from Santa Cruz, how is it you didn't end up in San Salvador?' asked the man of the house.

'I must have missed it. I don't know which way I came or didn't, the fact is I never passed through San Salvador or even saw it.'

'Not to worry,' intervened the old woman, 'my grandson here'll set you in the direction of Cezar and from there, by means of Portovello, you'll soon make it to Reborica.'

The conversation that followed is easy enough for anybody to imagine.

'Come on, woman, give this man something to eat…'

'Not to worry, I brought plenty of food with me…'

'Not at all. That food will come in handy for the return journey…'

The fact is it wasn't long before my father was dining 'competently', as the men in Cepelo are wont to say: a little ham on some homemade bread while two chorizos wrapped in cabbage leaves slowly roasted in the embers, in between the ashes and flames. After that, a slab of well-cured Manchego cheese, all washed down with a jug of wine that nestled close to the fire.

No doubt my father had one eye on the chorizo and another on the girl, he can't have been much older than she was, because it wasn't long before the young ones were sent off to bed.

And that was when they first heard the wolf: three howls, one long and high-pitched followed by two shorter ones.

'That wretched creature's out there again,' said the old woman.

'Do they often come down here?' asked my father.

'It's the first time I've heard them this year,' replied the man, 'but they've been hanging about for days, so I'm told.'

'Well, it's a good thing I found your house in time…'

'They also go down to Reborica each winter,' remarked the old woman. 'They descend from Cordal de Montouto and the Serpent's Cave and gather there, I've heard it can be frightening to spend the winter in some of the more isolated houses. Especially after what happened – there are still living souls who remember the affair.'

'What affair?' asked my father, who was always keen to get hold of a new story.

'You mean to say, after all those visits to Reborica, you've never been told the tale of Isaura?'

'I don't recall having heard it before.'

'Well, you won't go from here until I've told it to you myself, I know it well, my late departed husband was from Gallado, same as Isaura herself, God forgive her.'

'Please go ahead. I have often been in Cambás, right next to Gallado, but have never heard the story before.'

'This affair didn't take place in Gallado, that was where the girl was from, it all happened not far from Ponte de Aranga. There was a house there, a good house. The man was widowed early on, but until he died at a ripe old age, it was he who controlled what went on there, even though he had a married son who, with his wife, did most of the work on the estate. A fine holding it was, there's been threshing there that's gone on for eight days in succession! They could fill granaries and barns with wheat and rye, the like of which was never seen for leagues around.

'This couple had only the one son. This boy was the apple of his grandfather's eye, you might say he was crazy about him, something that's hard to accept in a man who almost single-handedly raised three children of his own, but the fact is he lost his head over that grandson of his. He even wanted him to study, something that never occurred to him when it came to his own children. So the boy was taken out of the local village school and sent to a boarding school in Coruña. You wouldn't believe the number of journeys the old man made just so he could see that little boy! Every now and then, off he'd go, and the boy can't have been sixteen when his grandfather was already spending a couple of days there, taking him out on the town and even a-whoring.

'It didn't take long for Silvestre, he had been named that after his grandfather, to acquire a taste for the good life; he never studied or did anything at all. The fact is he can't have been twenty and he was home again, with not even a high-school diploma to show for it, but he didn't want to work the land and help maintain the holding that would one day be his. As if he understood it would be enough to see him out and a lifetime wouldn't be enough to deplete it, the boy devoted himself to hunting by day and having fun at night. He could always rely on company, the old man made sure he had cash in his pocket and, where real friends were lacking, there were always hangers-on to take their place.

'The boy's father adopted a different outlook and expression as time went by and that good-for-nothing didn't lift a finger, whether it was a workday or the start of a holiday, it didn't matter much to him. I'm just supposing, but I imagine the boy's father searched for some kind of sin that was the reason for him to deserve a son like that, because neither he nor the old man had ever shied away from work, although they had plenty of capital. He wasn't stupid, however, he blamed the old man for the way he'd treated his grandson and apparently said to him one day,

"You made him like this, so why don't you try hitching him up to the cart if you think you're able…?"

'The general opinion was that something must have gone down in the house because the young man stopped hanging out with others and hitting the town in Coruña. Yes, he was seen to go hunting as always and to greet the day a good distance from home, having been in some tavern, but normally on his own. This wasn't the case. The thing is he'd taken a liking to women and didn't want people finding out about his shenanigans unless he chose to tell them, so he shared what he wanted and kept the rest to himself.

'I have to admit that Silvestre was by far the best-looking man for miles around. I never met him, but in my poor late husband's house there was a portrait of him with two sisters of my father-in-law's father, and he was a real looker. In appearance, his hair was light chestnut brown and wavy, his eyes a little green, and he was six and a half foot to say the least. A good-looking man if ever there was one. Apparently he was also talkative, witty and cheerful, it was spring where he was all year round. So it's hardly surprising the women went after him like bees to honey.

'If we're to believe the things that are said, he left no honour unsullied, no plate unlicked, even if it was just the ordinary plate of some good, honest gentleman. He set no limits to his affairs except those that were dictated by his own whim.

'So it was, like a cat on heat, he ended up in Gallado. It certainly wasn't the first time he'd been in those parts, everybody knew him. But it so turned out, on a night like this, he sought shelter in the house of a family from Revoldás. They were people like us, they ate every day, but never threshed late, since new bread is needed early. This family from Revoldás had three daughters, God hadn't wanted to give them a son, but they didn't need one, the eldest daughter had married one of the best and hardest-working men in the parish. The middle daughter had got married in Vilares, and the youngest was Isaura, who must have been about twenty.

'Silvestre warmed himself by the fire, but couldn't take his eyes off that dainty Isaura, who was as pretty as honeysuckle. Pale-faced and shapely, intelligent and outspoken, not like the rest of us, who went around gazing at the tips of our toes if there was a man anywhere nearby who wasn't already an acquaintance.

'Knowing what Silvestre was like, I'm quite sure he left that house, swearing to return soon. The wretched man certainly carried out his intention.

'A few months after that, Isaura became pregnant. She told Silvestre, who gave his word there and then that he would marry her. I don't know whether he included this as a condition or simply talked her into it, but the fact is the two of them left for Coruña early one morning and came back again the same night. After that, nobody ever saw Silvestre in Gallado again.

'Shortly afterwards, it became known that Silvestre was going to marry another girl at Candlemas. Isaura shut herself up at home and withered away as flowers do when they see summer has upped sticks and left. She still had enough strength in her, however, to go down to Ponte de Aranga on the day of the wedding. Those who saw her say she waited on the bridge for the bride and bridegroom, the best man, maid of honour and other guests to arrive. As you know, the church is within sight of the bridge. It seems she was as yellow as wax, but as upright and self-assured as a lady. When she judged the time was right, she entered the churchyard and positioned herself next to the door. As the bride and bridegroom were coming out, she went up to Silvestre and spat at him, loud enough for him to hear, "You owe me a child. Now you'll see how you pay me for it." And with that she pushed her way through the crowd and took the path that leads around the church.

'That same night, Isaura was found hanging from a chestnut tree. My father-in-law's father was one of those who took down the body and he said it weighed almost nothing at all, like a handful of straw. The priest didn't want to give her burial in the cemetery, so she was buried at night outside the cemetery wall. In March that year, the wolves came down and dug in the hole until they opened the coffin. By the time people got there, the coffin was empty except for the shroud Isaura had been wearing, which was all in tatters. They shut the coffin up again with the remains of the shroud and, on top of the earth they threw in, put a heavy stone so that no one would be able to rummage around in there again.

'After that, given that he was now married, you might have thought Silvestre would change his life, but nothing of the sort. He took his wife home, the old man had died by now and just his parents were left, and seemingly abandoned her. Like those children who set their eyes on something and won't stop until they get it, and then, when they've got it, they take it home and never give it any more attention. And bear in mind the girl he had married was exceedingly pretty, of quite a different caste to Isaura. Her name was Luciana, and she had an angled face, like a piece of wood before it's been sanded down. Slightly prominent cheeks over which shone two black eyes like the beads of a jet rosary, with eyelashes that were long and thin like threads of silk, a pretty nose, not too big, a mouth with well-delineated lips that would have been on the large side had there been a bit more to it. Only the chin was a little small for that face, all of which was framed by hair as dark as night that coursed down the sides like a waterfall of ocean waves. A touch shorter than he was, she had a strong, robust, but very feminine body. I saw her once in Coruña, I had been taken to see the lung doctor when I was very little and we bumped into her on the Cantón. What a pretty, upright, elegant old lady!

'Well, this buck, with a jewel like that at home, continued chasing after other women, no doubt trying to inflict further misfortune, as if the damage he'd caused wasn't enough. His parents, however, felt reassured because their daughter-in-law was formal and harder-working than most; even when she became pregnant, she carried on helping out almost until it was time for her to give birth.

'The winter that followed Isaura's death was particularly harsh. In Santos, it was colder than anybody could remember, while in Santa Lucía the wolves came down from Cordal and the Serpent's Cave. They were famished and attacked any animal that was left outside; they ate this dog we had, which was as large as a calf and very fierce. One morning, it turned up dead, half devoured by the wolves. The men went after them, and one of those who liked to join them was Silvestre. It wasn't that they had caused him any losses or made him afraid; he didn't seem to be afraid of anything, and losses at home never made him lose any sleep, he was just fond of hunting, of pursuing and harrying a prey until he caught it.

'They killed plenty of them and paraded them through the villages, where everybody gave them something.

'But there was this one pack that even the best hunters couldn't locate. It seemed almost always to come down somewhere between Cambás and Cordal de Montouto, which is why they called that the She-Wolf's Gully. There were six or seven large animals in the pack, some of them almost six feet from nose to tail. The men spent whole nights watching out for them; they were spotted climbing the She-Wolf's Ridge. Even from a distance, they could be seen to stop and huddle together, as if reaching an agreement, it's the only explanation there is. They then went their separate ways. The hunters prepared to stake them out, but no sooner had they set eyes on one of them than the other wolves would surround them, jump on top of them so they couldn't use their weapons, either out of fear of wounding some companion or because the wolves landed on the men in such a way it was all they could do to withdraw without getting bitten. They then seemed suddenly to disappear, nobody could say how or where they'd done this. It wasn't just once or twice, it happened lots of times; the men became familiar with that pack and talked about it at home and in the tavern.

'It seems the lead animal was a female with eyes like two red-hot irons. It was the fiercest of them all; it would turn up in front of somebody, plant its feet on the ground, howl and bare its teeth without ever taking a step backwards.

'People were horrified when they heard about it and barred their doors and windows as soon as it started getting dark. The wolves, sensing their fear, came down more often and approached the houses. To start with, they would come up very slowly, without making any noise, but as soon as people realized they were there, someone in the house sensed there was a wolf about, they would start howling and scratching at the doors like madmen.

'Around Christmas, Silvestre's wife gave birth to a baby boy; people said it was a good time for him to be born because he was as bonny as the Child Jesus that St Anthony holds in his arms. The doctor and midwife were forced to sleep over. The wolves spent the whole night prowling around the house, howling like crazy and scratching at the doors. Silvestre fired shots through the windows, but didn't hit any.

'It stopped snowing for a few days, and Silvestre started gathering people so they could go looking for the pack. They would head towards the Gully by day, some along one side of the river and others along the other. They spent weeks and weeks scouring Cordal de Montouto and the Serpent's Cave; they killed some, all males except for one female, but it wasn't the one they were after, it was smaller.

'On the night of February the first, somebody saw this huge wolf in Ponte de Aranga. Someone else sensed the presence of wolves in Muniferral. News of this soon spread and everybody, for more than a league on either side of the Mandeo, shut themselves up at home.

'The men came together where today there's a little square behind the parish church of Aranga. Silvestre soon appeared, riding the mare from his house, and started organizing people. He was just doing this when two wolves raced by as if they'd come from the river. "There they are!" The first shots of many that were heard that night rang out. The men went after them with the dogs. The wolves climbed in the direction of Rilleira, where Silvestre's house was, with greater agility and speed than the men and dogs, but even so the latter didn't give up the chase. Sometimes, the dogs would catch up with them, but the wolves would turn around and, as soon as they bared their teeth, the poor dogs would back down. In an attempt to cut them off, they decided to separate into groups. Some saw a wolf passing in front of them on a cart-track. The others climbed this slope, sensing there might be wolves at the top of the ravine.

'When the men, following their tracks, reached Rilleira, they had already killed two wolves, which they immediately recognized as belonging to the pack they had been chasing all winter. Men recognize the face of a wolf when they've been on its tail for a long time, even if they've never had a good sight of it or seen it for long. Up there, among the houses, they cornered and killed another two, but the three that were left, which included the she-wolf in charge of the pack, managed to escape more than once.

'Finally, at the entrance to a chestnut grove there was in that parish, they saw the three animals go in. They charged in after them and saw them slip through the trees and start climbing the hill. They were running almost side by side. The men sent the dogs after them, and the wolves split up, two heading towards the east over cultivated land, taking the dogs with them, and the third continuing up the mountain.

'As the men followed the dogs in pursuit of the wolves that were running aimlessly now over open countryside, the she-wolf turned back to Rilleira, passed in between the houses and didn't stop running until it came to Silvestre's house. From a window upstairs, Luciana saw its eyes gleaming in the darkness like two bright sparks as it slowed to a walk before arriving. It went twice around the house, scratched at the door and was seen no more; it had entered a lean-to next to the house and from there passed into the kitchen. Luciana, as if sensing what it was up to, ran downstairs to confront it, she put up a resistance, the animal bared its teeth and leaped on top of her, the woman fell backwards and crashed to the kitchen floor. She came to just in time to see the she-wolf jump clean over her body and head outside, carrying the little child in its mouth. She started shouting, the in-laws came down, but it took them a while to understand what was going on because their daughter-in-law couldn't explain herself properly.

'In its flight, the wolf didn't head towards the mountain, it took to the tracks and passed like lightning in front of the men coming back. They urged on their dogs and raced after it. The beast leaped over some stones, entered the threshing floor of a house, crossed it and sought refuge in a barn. The men with rifles arrived, and the owner of the house showed them where it was hiding. They approached the barn, but were still ten or fifteen feet away when the she-wolf appeared in the doorway and confronted them. The dogs made straight for the wolf, barking and harassing it, but it refused to back down. For fear of wounding the dogs, the men preferred not to use their weapons. Silvestre went straight around the barn, shut one of the leaves of the door at the same time as somebody else shut the other, ran over to a haystack, grabbed a handful of hay, set fire to it, opened the door half a foot and threw the burning torch inside. In less time than it takes to tell you, the whole barn was up in flames and in amidst all the crackling of the fire could be heard these howls that sent cracks shooting up the walls of heaven. Silvestre laughed like a madman, swearing and cursing the wolf.

'At this point, Luciana and Silvestre's father appeared, shouting like souls out of hell. Silvestre went over to them, and they told him what had happened. He turned around in a fit of madness and, with eyes as wide as those of Our Lady of Sorrows, ran towards the barn and went inside; it was all lamentation when there was this horrifying scream from Silvestre; after that, only silence.

'By the time they'd put out the fire and entered the barn, child, wolf and man formed an indistinguishable mass on the ground.'

The old woman fell silent, staring at my father.

'And that's the end of this sad, sad story. Silvestre's parents died soon after, and Luciana moved to Coruña, where she passed away and was buried some time ago. Silvestre's cousins inherited the holding, which they split up and sold. All that's left of the house are the bare walls in amidst the brambles.'

The next day, my father made it to Reborica and asked about the story. The people there had heard it from their elders just as the old woman had told it to him, and he to me.

Happy Death Day

He would have liked

to be able to remember everything he'd done on the day he received the first letter, but it was so many years ago he'd forgotten most of the details. It wasn't so important, nothing from before could be changed. What had happened would accompany him forever; successes and failures formed an indivisible whole that was called 'the immovable past'. He should direct all his energy towards the time that lay ahead, especially now he sensed there wasn't much of it. That morning, in the strange post, he'd received the same envelope without a return address that had arrived on the same day the previous year and the year before that. It was one of those so-called mourning envelopes with a black ribbon running all around the edge. Inside was a card with a similar black border and the following text: 'Happy Death Day!' In the bottom right-hand corner, the date.

It was the third year he'd received this card and he realized it would be the last.

Everything had started one day when he got home and pulled out of the postbox an envelope that struck him as strange, it reminded him of his childhood, both because it was a mourning envelope and because of how it was made; it was one of those textured envelopes that have the feel of light cloth. He opened it and was able to read, on mourning paper, a text that had been written in well-shaped letters, leaning slightly to the right, a little pretentious in the curves that extended above and below the line, and that said:

> *Dear sir,*
>
> *In the same way as people congratulate their friends when it's the anniversary of the day they were born, so I send you my congratulations because today is the anniversary of the day you are going to die. It may sound like a joke, but I can assure you it isn't. I know perfectly well that you will die on today's date (please allow me not to tell you the year, everything will come in time). I understand that, to start with, this could appear to be bad news, but once you have recovered from the initial shock and have thought about it a little, you will realize this is a privilege more than anything else, because it will enable you to make preparations that few are allowed to carry out, since men these days have started living as if they were never going to die. Nothing is so certain or sure for a man than his own death, which makes other things that could happen to us somewhat less relevant.*
>
> *Allow me to take my leave, for now, by wishing you a very Happy Death Day!*

That was all. There was no signature or mark of any kind. Just the date of the day when he had received the letter – not the day it had been written, but the very day on which he was reading it.

In effect, he took it as a joke in bad taste, although he kept the letter with the intention of attempting to compare the handwriting with that of his colleagues at work to see if he could discover who possessed such a macabre sense of humour. Using all kinds of excuses, he managed to get hold of samples of handwriting from the people he knew and every night would compare them to that in the letter, but none of them could be declared a match.

Little by little, he started forgetting about the affair until one day there was a knock at the door and a man appeared with a bunch of flowers in his name. There was a ribbon attached to it, on which were printed the following words: 'I HAVEN'T FORGOTTEN YOU'. This was getting beyond a joke – he was quite sure by now it was just a joke.

Since nothing else happened, he came to the conclusion that the joker had grown tired and started putting the affair out of his mind. All the same, as the same day the following year approached, he began to feel nervous. He was worried and ill at ease. He had the sensation he would like to delay the passage of time and started doing everything very slowly: he worked slowly, walked slowly, ate slowly… He would have preferred to stop behaving in this way, but couldn't, it was something that was superior to him.

The day arrived. He didn't go to work and spent the whole morning watching out for the postman. When he saw him through the window, he rushed outside and went to meet him. From a distance, he could see in amidst the bundle of letters the postman was carrying one that had a black border. He felt a stabbing pain in his chest. The postman, seeing him there, sorted through the letters and handed him two of them: the one in the mourning envelope and another. As he took them, his hands were shaking like grass. He started walking, running almost, towards the house and, once inside, he sank into an armchair and gazed at the mourning envelope. He turned it round and round, not daring to open it. He placed it on the table and couldn't take his eyes off it. He got up, wandered about the house, but always ended up back at the table where he had left the envelope, his eyes fixed on it, as if endeavouring to guess its contents without having to open it. He thought about ripping it up unopened, but couldn't bring himself to do this.

It had to be a joke, nobody knows the day someone is going to die, unless they're planning to kill that person, in which case they'll make sure not to give any warning signs so the person doesn't take precautions. The best thing was to throw the envelope in the bin. Or to open it – it didn't matter now whether he read it or not.

In the end, he opened it. It also contained a letter on mourning paper, but this one was shorter:

Dear sir,

For the second year running, I address myself to you to wish you a Happy Death Day! Please be informed I will only greet you another two times on this date, but you will still hear from me and have proof of my presence and vigilance.

Have a nice day.

It also had no signature and was dated that day.

Having read the letter, he felt suddenly dizzy. He flopped into the armchair. His arms on the armrests, his hands hanging down like those of a dead man. His head thrown back, his face as pale as the wall. Once he started feeling a little better, his mind began to function again. Who could it be? This wasn't a joke anymore, this was something that had to be taken seriously. He could always go and file a complaint, but they'd probably just tell him it was a joke and he shouldn't worry. He had to come up with a plan that didn't depend on others.

Given that he had no family, the first thing would be to change his place of residence. This is what he did. He resigned from work without giving any explanations or sharing anything about his future destiny and left the city. He rented a property in another town and more or less shut himself up in the house – he only came out when it was necessary and had no dealings with anybody. He didn't receive any mail, the postman didn't even know of his existence.

He had been living there for three months when the postman knocked at the door and handed him a small envelope. It was one of those so-called mourning envelopes. It was in his name and had the correct address. He opened it and pulled out a commemorative card in the form of a diptych, with Christ Crucified on the outside and Our Lady of Sorrows on the back cover. Inside, beneath a cross, had been printed his name followed by the fateful date on which he always received his death-day letters; but the year wasn't this one, or the next, it was the one after that. Underneath, the letters 'RIP'. All the other texts were prayers in which his soul was commended to God.

He was sure by now that it was death sending him these letters. This tied in with what was happening: death will always find you, wherever you may be. You can hide from anything, even from yourself with deception and forgetfulness, but not from death. It was clear, therefore, that death was responsible and, faced by this conclusion, there was nothing to do but give in. There was no point in kicking up a fuss.

This thought left him feeling unarmed. It wasn't that he'd put up much of a fight – that was just because he hadn't discovered the right way to rebel; he had the sensation that with the change of residence, especially now this measure had proved to be in vain, he'd done all he could. This new thought that filled his head was that it had been given to him to know his destiny in advance and there was nothing he could do about it.

His depression lasted for weeks, during which he barely slept or ate, he simply entertained vain thoughts – thoughts about the futility of fighting destiny and death. He was more and more convinced there was nothing he could do.

Little by little, he recovered as much tranquillity as he was capable of recovering in such an abnormal situation. This permitted him to reflect on a possible means of evading destiny. There could be a way ahead, and he had to seek it out as best he could.

He disappeared from the town without saying anything to anybody and moved to a large city. He would have many more opportunities there to pass completely unnoticed and to fight against this destiny that had been given him with a fixed date. He tried to live as freely as possible. He was no longer tied to all those things that seemed to him to deprive him of liberty. With no fixed abode, no bank account, no name or ID, no timetable or obligations, he could resist all the prearranged destinies that had been imposed on him.

Now, however, he had just received the final letter. It had been handed to him by a waiter as he was drinking his morning coffee in a café he had never entered before. The waiter said it had been given to him by a woman, who had asked him to deliver it. The man asked what the woman was like; the waiter said she was middle-aged and dressed in a blue overcoat. He rushed outside, but couldn't find her. He walked slowly along the pavement until he came to a park. He sat down on a bench and opened the envelope.

The letter was in his name, a name he hadn't used for some time or told anyone. He pulled out the mourning paper and noticed the date – he had only a year left. At least he wouldn't be getting any more letters with their ironic congratulations. There was no doubt he was starting the last year of his life. What was he going to do?

During that year, he decided to live as if these letters had never existed, the way any normal human being lives: he knows he has to die, but doesn't know when. He turned into someone who never did anything unless he was sure he felt like it and wanted to. He even came across as irresolute when that wasn't the case – it's just that he would think about doing something in a particular way and then end up doing the opposite. That said, before taking a decision, he would weigh it up a lot, consider all possible consequences of his actions. He was like a chess player who thinks about the many responses, his own and those of his opponent, that can follow the move he is contemplating.

The day arrived. The night before, he didn't sleep a wink. In the morning, he went outside, but not without paying for the following night so they would reserve his room; since he had no possessions, he had to meet the cost of each night's stay in advance.

He wandered aimlessly about the streets, as he had been doing ever since he decided to live in the anonymity of the city. It was winter and very cold. In that city that was further east than the lands he had been born and lived in, it always got darker earlier than he expected at this time of year. With the darkness, the cold increased, and then there was the likelihood of a frost. It wasn't pleasant being outside, so he decided to head back to the guest house. It was some distance from where he was, but at least he would warm his feet.

He didn't want to think how little remained of the day he was due to die, little more than six hours. He preferred to think most of the day had already passed and he was still alive. In actual fact, the time that had passed seemed very distant in his memory while the time that remained seemed very long and very present. In order to die, all that was required was for his heart to stop, and this can happen in a moment, in a thousandth of a second. Even less – in the infinitely small space there is between being alive and dead. In a time that is immeasurable.

Suddenly, he stopped walking. Why did he have to go back to the guest house where he'd slept the previous night? Just because he'd paid for the room in the morning? That meant he was doing something that seemed to have been dictated by an inevitable destiny. Well, he was capable of avoiding this: he would go and sleep in a different guest house. It might be another kind of destiny, but he had in mind now the thing he liked best about his new situation: the freedom to choose. He chose: he would go somewhere different.

He passed in front of a house and, on the wall next to the door, saw a blue sign with an 'H' and two stars. He went inside and asked for a room; he paid, they gave him the key, and he started walking along this long corridor, paying attention to the numbers on the doors until he reached number 17. He put the key in the lock and entered the room. He switched on the light. It was a small room with a bed, a night table, a wardrobe with a mirrored door and a wicker chair. There was also a washbasin. The room had a narrow window that looked out onto such a small yard he felt he could almost reach out with his hand and touch the opposite window.

There were five hours left before the day ended. He lay on the bed without getting undressed; he thought if he was going to die, he didn't want them finding a naked corpse, he preferred to be dressed for when the police and coroner came. Waiting for time to pass is not one of the most entertaining 'pastimes' there is in this world, but he had nothing else to do that day but wait for time to pass and then see what would happen. Lying on top of the bed, the same question kept going round inside his head: what was the outcome going to be? All the same, his mind did wander to other things; for example, he spent lots of time gazing at the lamp, then trailing his eyes over the ceiling, where he could see these very bright rings sometimes, and other times the filament of the lamp.

In a church, a clock struck nine. He hadn't heard it strike eight. It seemed this game of staring at the light was a good way for time to pass without him realizing. That said, it was no relief to him that time was passing without him realizing, because that meant there was less of it left.

He suddenly leaped off the bed. What was he doing there, waiting for his hour to come like a man who has been sentenced to death and is helpless to change his destiny? He went out into the corridor and passed in front of the man who had given him the key without saying a word. In less than a minute, he was back in the street.

In the year he'd spent in that city, this would be the first night he wouldn't sleep in a hotel, but any place will do for dying, he thought to himself. The clock of another church struck ten. He carried on walking, and one of those clocks that seem to flick through the leaves of a book of time showed him two 1s, followed by two 0s, the latter separated from the former by a colon. He had one hour left. He glanced at his watch: fifty-nine minutes. He looked at it again, and now it was two minutes past eleven. He consulted it one minute later. Then he pulled it off his wrist and threw it in a bin. He carried on walking aimlessly and ended up in this square that was new, but small and poorly illuminated on account of these cleverly designed lamps that pointed down so much all they did was light up their own bases. He went and sat on a bench. What time was it now? He didn't care. If the Grim Reaper was coming, then let him come, he'd done everything he could so as not to be found. With his hands in his coat pockets, his legs outstretched and his chin resting on his chest, he settled down. He felt well. Apparently this is how one feels shortly before dying. A woman came and sat next to him and asked him the time. Without looking at her, he replied that he didn't have a watch. He thought she might be a prostitute who was in the habit of opening negotiations by asking the time.

'It's after twelve,' said the woman.

On hearing this, he turned to face the woman.

'What did you say?'

'I said it's after twelve.'

'Are you sure?'

'I am. I was just passing in front of that green building when I heard the town-hall clock strike twelve.'

The man clasped his head in his hands and started mumbling to himself, 'I knew it couldn't be true, it had to be a joke in poor taste,' and things like that.

'No, it wasn't a joke. It was most definitely true,' affirmed the woman without looking at him.

He seemed not to hear what the woman was saying, so she got up and started walking slowly across the square. She was just about to disappear from sight when he seemed to comprehend what it was she had said and went running after her. He managed to come alongside her just as she was entering a street that had no more illumination than that of the signs and the lights in the shop windows. Before one of these, he grabbed hold of the woman's arm and pulled her round so she was facing him. She was a young woman, but with the air of a great lady; upright, with squared shoulders and breasts pointing firmly at the man's chest, she stared at him almost arrogantly. Her face was extremely pale, although it could have been as a result of the light, which was very white and lit up one side of her face while the other remained in darkness; her eyes were clear, almost transparent, and a little bloodshot.

'What did you say?'

'I said so many things…'

'You said it wasn't a joke…'

'No, it wasn't. You were supposed to die today.'

'How do you know that?'

'Because I'm the one who sent you those letters.'

'What's that? You're the one who put me through those four years of hell? What on earth for?'

'It isn't easy to explain. It was given to me to know that you would die today, and so I informed you. Sometimes I do it one way, sometimes another, but that's not the point.'

'So, why is it I haven't died?'

'Because it doesn't always happen. It's easy to get it right with those who just let themselves go, who don't do anything to change their lives. But with those who make use of their freedom to take decisions, who are capable of accepting the consequences of their actions because they're the ones who dictate them, it isn't easy. That's what you did. You went from being a man who allowed himself to be swallowed up by routine, as if all your actions had been programmed and had nothing to do with you, to acting independently, to taking your life and destiny in your own hands. At this point, everything that had been written about your destiny first became bleary and then disappeared, your life went back to being a blank page. That is why your destiny hasn't happened, because men who behave as such invent and write their own destinies.'

The man fell silent for a moment, staring at the woman in front of him, who remained more or less as expressionless as before.

'And who might you be?'

'I'm just what is left of the person I once was: a woman who was unhappy because she let her destiny take place without doing anything to prevent it. Now I have to wander the world in an attempt to alter my final destiny… and that is what I am about.'

Having said this, she started walking again. The man watched her leave. Suddenly, he remembered there was still something he wanted to ask and he ran after her to question her again. She was some distance away, so he quickened his pace and took her by the arm.

'What should I do now?'

The woman turned to face him.

'Listen, sir, do whatever you like, and stop bothering people in the street.'

I Am Afraid…

When there's a knock on the door at night.
Of being alone when I don't want to be.
Of being amidst lots of people.
Of ending up all alone in the world.
Of never dying.
Of dying too soon.
Of dying foolishly in a road accident.
Of becoming useless.
Of going mad.
Of something happening to my family.
Of those I love not loving me in return.
Of losing interest in the things I enjoy.
Of having always to live in a city.
Of there not being any flowers.
Of there being no animals in the wild.
Of not being able to gaze at the stars at night.
Of not being able to gaze at a landscape in autumn.
Of the sea (when at sea).

Of looking up at the sky one day and not seeing any birds.
Of there not being any trout in the rivers.
Of having to go to war.
Of war, even if I don't have to go.
Of wretched souls.
Of those who always tell the truth.
Of those who always lie.
Of being hungry.
Of horror stories.
Of horror films.
Of having to go to the dentist.
Of travelling by plane.
Of not being afraid of anything.
Of being very afraid.
When it's been an age since anybody knocked at my door.
Of...

Read more fiction in English from Small Stations Press:

Xabier P. DoCampo, THE BOOK OF IMAGINARY JOURNEYS

Inspired by Italo Calvino's Invisible Cities, *The Book of Imaginary Journeys* by Xabier P. DoCampo follows in the tradition of great travel literature that began with Homer's *Odyssey*. It purports to be the transcription of two travel journals written by a certain X.B.R., in which the Traveller gives as objective a description as he can of the cities and kingdoms he visits. So it is he comes to a city you can only visit for three days or where you cannot fall asleep, a city balanced on the fine point of a diamond or rotating on a water wheel, a city whose inhabitants are all tree-dwelling women or descended from birds, a city where the tombstones are inscribed not with the names of the deceased but with the titles of their favourite books, a city where money is only valid for a year, where none of its inhabitants can go fishing because all the rods have been turned into soldiers' lances, whose ministers are made to wear nooses as a warning to stay clean... The Traveller records songs, proverbs and remedies he hears along the way and describes some of the people he meets – a woman who conducts imaginary orchestras, a man who loves the earth so much he would like to plough it with a pair of unicorns, another searching for a treasure guarded by seven keys... Like translation, travel is a return to the source, the point of departure. What the Traveller takes away from the experience is what he has learned.

ISBN 978-954-384-063-2

Agustín Fernández Paz, NOTHING REALLY MATTERS IN LIFE MORE THAN LOVE

The ten stories in this magnificent collection 'all talk of the importance of love, that feeling that can transform us more deeply than any other, and also of its absence, the void it leaves in people when the twists and turns of life make it impossible.' So the author, Agustín Fernández Paz, writes in his afterword. A banker who, bored of the company of other directors, frequents a bookshop and is introduced to works she has never read before; a young man who falls in love with the daughter of the owner of the garage where he works; a man and a dog who continue to seek out the company of the Woman he loved; a couple who endure a freak accident, but only one survives; a woman who recalls her first, anxious physical contact with her boyfriend; a man who is proud of his collection of matchboxes; another who finds passport photos of the woman of his dreams on the pavement; the country house and its long-kept secrets; a woman whose life could have been so different had she followed the inclinations of her heart; and the man who comes up with the ingenious idea of advertising not services, but the openings of books that have transformed his life. There is in this work an analysis of the power of love over our lives, love that is requited and love that is left behind. There is also, as the author points out, a celebration of the positive impact that reading can have in our lives, and Fernández Paz very deliberately sets out to provide pointers to some of his favourite creators: Auster, Kafka, Pamuk and Rivas, Éluard, Neruda, Valcárcel and Valente, Hicks, Kar-wai and Wenders… Readers will be able not only to sink into the charming prose of one of Galicia's most famous writers, but also to equip themselves with a to-do list of other authors. *Nothing Really Matters in Life More Than Love* received the 2008 Spanish National Book Award and is beautifully illustrated in colour by Pablo Auladell.

ISBN 978-954-384-086-1

Teresa Moure, BLACK NIGHTSHADE

Einés Andrade is a doctoral student whose studies center on the figure of the French philosopher René Descartes. But when she is only seven or eight, she is sent to the attic for calling her great-grandmother a monkey, and there she discovers a hutch, a large chest, from which emanate the scents of various herbs and fruits. She also discovers private papers belonging to Queen Christina of Sweden and a certain Hélène Jans, a herbalist and healer of Amsterdam. Digging deeper, she discovers that the two women shared a common passion. In 1649, Christina of Sweden invited Descartes to her court to give her lessons in philosophy, but he was reputed to have caught pneumonia and died in February, 1650. Before that, he had an affair—only once, as he claimed—with the maid of the bookseller in whose house he was staying in Amsterdam, Hélène Jans. She became pregnant and gave birth to their daughter, Francine, who died at the age of five in 1640. Fifteen years later, Queen Christina and Hélène meet to exchange impressions and ease their nostalgia. They strike up a correspondence in which Christina urges Hélène to continue her work on an artificial language, a language that can be easily learned and will serve to promote communication among different nations and prevent war. Hélène also puts together a recipe book, called *Book of Women*, in which she gives various remedies that can be used to alleviate pain in childbirth, to improve one's appearance, to attract a lover… Before she dies, she hands down her knowledge, the recipe book and her private papers, to her adopted daughter, Agnes, a distant ancestor of Einés's. Einés decides to abandon all research on rationalism and to devote her time to writing an account of these women whom Time has forgotten. *Black Nightshade*, which could just as easily have been titled *Chest in the Attic*, *Patchwork Quilt* or *Scent of Raspberries*, is an emblematic work by a leading writer of her generation, Teresa Moure, and was awarded the Xerais Prize for Novels in 2005.

ISBN 978-954-384-085-4

Anxos Sumai, THAT'S HOW WHALES ARE BORN

A young woman, who has left Galicia to go and study marine biology in Mexico (Baja California), is recalled to Galicia when it is found out that her mother is very sick. Her aunt would like her to sign some papers agreeing to take over the family business and renouncing her Mexican studies and emotional ties that she has forged in her new life. However, returning to Galicia and renewing her family ties is not exactly what the woman wants. Her mother has shut herself in her room for the last year, and relations between them have always been strained. She received more affection from a nanny, Felisa, and better advice from her uncle, Cándido. There is also an older brother, Ramón, a larger-than-life figure who has left an indelible mark in the lives of those around him, and an absent father. Will the woman's visit to see her sick mother turn out to be permanent, and will it soothe any of the festering wounds in her psyche, wounds that she has buried beneath her marine studies and a relationship with her one-time tutor? *That's How Whales Are Born* is a return to our origins, a search into the usefulness of stirring up past memories and seeking reconciliation.

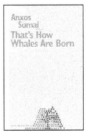

ISBN 978-954-384-073-1

For an up-to-date list of our publications, please visit
www.smallstations.com